A Royal Makeover

Adapted by Lara Bergen

Based on the Teleplay by Annie DeYoung

Based on the Story by David Morgasen and Annie DeYoung

DISNEY PRESS

NEW YORK

Copyright © 2009 Disney Enterprises, Inc.
All rights reserved. Published by Disney Press, an imprint of Disney Book Group.
No part of this book may be reproduced or transmitted in any form or by any means,
electronic or mechanical, including photocopying, recording, or by any information
storage and retrieval system, without written permission from the publisher.
For information address Disney Press, 114 Fifth Avenue, New York, New York 10011-5690.
Printed in the United States of America

First Edition
1 3 5 7 9 10 8 6 4 2
Library of Congress Control Number: 2009901207
ISBN 978-1-4231-2285-2

For more Disney Press fun, visit www.disneybooks.com
Visit DisneyChannel.com

Chapter 1

Once upon a time, in a kingdom called Costa Luna, there lived a princess named Rosalinda.

Rosalinda was kind and good and loved by all her people. After her father, the king, passed away, it was decided that she would be crowned queen. She was getting ready for her coronation, which was only one month away.

But an evil man named General Kane was also in Costa Luna. He was the ruler of another island nation—Costa Estrella. He wanted to rule Costa Luna, too.

General Kane went to the palace to watch the princess practice for the ceremony. He planned to capture her! Then he could be king of both countries.

Luckily, Rosalinda's mother, Sophia, knew what General Kane was planning. She had called the International Princess Protection Program, a secret agency that rescued princesses in trouble. Before General Kane could kidnap Rosalinda, the top agent in the program, Major Mason, rescued her.

Mr. Mason took Rosalinda to the Princess Protection Program headquarters. The director explained that Rosalinda would be hidden in a safe place after she had been disguised.

"As of this moment, you are no longer a princess," the director told her. "From now on, you are Rosie Gonzalez, an average American girl."

Rosalinda was given a haircut and new clothes.

Then Mr. Mason took her somewhere General Kane would never think to look: his cabin in Louisiana.

Mr. Mason lived in Louisiana with his daughter, Carter, who was the same age as Rosalinda.

When Carter got home from school, Rosalinda was sitting in her bedroom. "Who are you?" Carter asked.

"Rosa . . . uh . . . Rosie?" Rosalinda said. "Major Mason gave me this room."

Rosie could tell that Carter was not happy. But all she cared about was staying safe until she could go home.

Back in Costa Luna, General Kane asked Sophia if she'd heard anything from Rosalinda.

"No," Sophia said coldly. "You will never be king of Costa Luna! Not as long as I am alive."

General Kane smiled. He believed he would be king. It was just a matter of time.

Sophia thought of her daughter, hidden somewhere far away. She hoped Rosalinda was safe.

Chapter 2

The next morning, Rosie went to school with Carter. She was nervous. In Costa Luna, she hadn't gone to high school. Tutors had come to the palace to teach her.

Rosie tried her best to fit in. But it wasn't easy.

In French class, she spoke the language better than the teacher. At lunch, she ate her hamburger with a knife and fork.

By the end of the day, Carter was frustrated with Rosie.

"She can't do it, Dad!" Carter yelled when they got home. "She can't act normal."

"I am normal," Rosie protested.

But as Rosie thought about her first day, she wondered if maybe she hadn't done so well at trying to fit in. She promised herself that she would do better tomorrow. Her life, and her country, depended on it.

Rosie got up early the next day. She wanted to show Carter that she could blend in like a regular American teenager. She found Carter in the Bait Shack.

"What is it you are doing?" she asked.

"Saturday chores," Carter said.

"Perhaps I could learn this," Rosie said as she watched Carter work.

Carter thought that was a good idea. She led Rosie to a large container of slimy worms. She told Rosie that they needed to be counted.

Rosie wrinkled her nose. Then she stuck her hand in the container and started to count.

That night, Rosie laughed with Mr. Mason as they ate their supper.

Carter frowned. "Must be nice to play peasant for a day," she said.

Rosie looked at Carter sadly. Then she left the room.

Carter sighed. She followed Rosie into her bedroom.

"You do not know me, Carter," Rosie said. "One month before my coronation, our palace was attacked. The man who invaded Costa Luna now holds my mother as a hostage. They told me becoming Rosie Gonzalez was the only way to keep her safe."

Carter felt terrible. She knew she had to give Rosie a second—and fair—chance.

Chapter 3

Carter decided to take Rosie bowling to teach her how to be a regular teenager. She helped Rosie get shoes and pick out a ball.

"Just do what I do," Carter told her.

Rosie gave it a try. She didn't know what she was doing. But she ended up knocking down every pin! Soon a crowd gathered around her, including some of the most popular kids in school.

Two of the girls, Chelsea and Brooke, realized something then. The homecoming queen election was coming up. And everyone really liked Rosie . . . she could win the crown!

Chelsea wanted the crown for herself. So she came up with a plan to make Rosie look bad.

She got Rosie a job at her father's yogurt shop. Then she texted everyone at school, telling them to go to the shop at the same time. Rosie was still learning how to make the perfect cone when everyone showed up. She couldn't keep up with the crowds and spilled yogurt everywhere.

That evening, Rosie sat on the pier with Carter. She told Carter more about her life in Costa Luna and about the kind of queen she would like to be someday.

"I want to make a difference," Rosie said.

"You're different from what I thought a princess would be," Carter said, grinning. "That's a good thing."

The next day at school, the principal announced the finalists for homecoming queen.

"Chelsea Barnes, Carter Mason, and Rosie Gonzalez!" he said.

Carter was stunned. She didn't think she would make a very good homecoming queen.

But Rosie disagreed. She showed Carter what the job of a true princess involved. It was about much more than tiaras and pretty dresses.

They read to children at the preschool. They tutored students in math and Spanish. They donated many things to the local thrift shop. And there, they found the perfect dresses for the homecoming dance.

A few days before the dance, Chelsea was in the gym decorating. Brooke came running up to her with a magazine. She showed Chelsea an article about a woman named Sophia, who was to marry General Kane. Beside the article was a photo of the woman and her daughter: *Princess* Rosalinda.

Chelsea smiled.

They took the article to Rosie.

"Drop the act," they told her. "We know all about you."

Rosie begged them not to tell her secret. Chelsea said they would only if Rosie gave up her homecoming crown.

"Fine," Rosie agreed. "You can have my crown. But not Carter's."

When Carter came home later, Rosie told her what had happened. "I have to leave, Carter," she said.

Carter knew Rosie wanted to save her mother and her country. But she also knew that General Kane would throw Rosie in jail if she returned to Costa Luna.

She asked Rosie to stay until the dance. Then she came up with a plan to save Rosie and Costa Luna.

Carter called Rosie's royal dressmaker, Señor Elegante, and asked him to make two dresses. She told him to tell General Kane where Rosie was, and that she'd be wearing a blue dress to the dance.

When the dresses arrived in the mail, Rosie was surprised. She couldn't believe Carter had done this for her!

The next night, Carter and Rosie went to the homecoming dance. They wore masks and their new dresses. Carter wore the blue one, and Rosie wore pink.

Soon it was time for the big announcement. "May I have your attention, please?" the principal said. "The Lake Monroe homecoming queen is . . . Princess Rosie Gonzalez!"

As Rosie took the stage to accept her crown, she searched the crowd for Carter. But she couldn't find her. Rosie didn't know it, but General Kane was there. And he had grabbed Carter, thinking she was the princess.

Rosie raced outside looking for Carter. She found her with General Kane. Just then, Mr. Mason and some other secret agents jumped out of a waiting helicopter and captured General Kane.

Rosie and Costa Luna were saved, all thanks to Carter's plan.

"I can't believe you did all this for me," Rosie said.

Carter shrugged. "That's what princesses do, right?" she said. "They do for others."

"You are truly a princess, Carter Mason." Rosie smiled.

It was finally safe for Rosie to return home to Costa Luna. She invited Carter and her father to come for her coronation ceremony, which would now only be a short time away.

The day of the ceremony, Sophia looked
on proudly as her daughter took her place as
Costa Luna's queen.

"Long live Queen Rosie!" Carter called out.

Rosalinda smiled. The kingdom of Costa
Luna was happy and peaceful once again.